W9-ATF-613

Each Puffin Easy-to-Read book has a color-coded reading level to make book selection easy for parents and children. Because all children are unique in their reading development, Puffin's three levels make it easy for teachers and parents to find the right book to suit each individual child's reading readiness.

Level 1: Short, simple sentences full of word repetition—plus clear visual clues to help children take the first important steps toward reading.

Level 2: More words and longer sentences for children just beginning to read on their own.

Level 3: Lively, fast-paced text—perfect for children who are reading on their own.

"Readers aren't born, they're made.
Desire is planted—planted by
parents who work at it."

—**Jim Trelease**, author of
The Read-Aloud Handbook

Digby and Kate

by Barbara Baker

pictures by
Marsha Winborn

PUFFIN BOOKS

for my mother and father
B.A.B.

PUFFIN BOOKS
Published by the Penguin Group
Penguin Books USA Inc., 375 Hudson Street, New York, New York 10014, U.S.A.
Penguin Books Ltd, 27 Wrights Lane, London W8 5TZ, England
Penguin Books Australia Ltd, Ringwood, Victoria, Australia
Penguin Books Canada Ltd, 10 Alcorn Avenue, Toronto, Ontario, Canada M4V 3B2
Penguin Books (N.Z.) Ltd, 182–190 Wairau Road, Auckland 10, New Zealand

Penguin Books Ltd, Registered Offices: Harmondsworth, Middlesex, England

First published in the United States of America by E.P. Dutton, 1988
Published in a Puffin Easy-to-Read edition, 1993

Text copyright © Barbara A. Baker, 1988
Illustrations copyright © Marsha Winborn, 1988
All rights reserved

LIBRARY OF CONGRESS CATALOGING-IN-PUBLICATION DATA
Baker, Barbara, 1947–
Digby and Kate / by Barbara Baker;
pictures by Marsha Winborn. p. cm.
Summary: Six episodes in the friendship of Digby the dog and Kate the cat,
who enjoy each other's company even when they have their differences
in such areas as catching a mouse or fixing lunch.
ISBN 0-14-036547-8
[1. Friendship—Fiction. 2. Cats—Fiction. 3. Dogs—Fiction.]
I. Winborn, Marsha, ill. II. Title.
PZ7.B16922Di 1993
[E]—dc20 93-6555 CIP AC

Puffin® and Easy-to-Read® are registered trademarks of Penguin Books USA Inc.
Printed in the United States of America

Except in the United States of America, this book is sold subject
to the condition that it shall not, by way of trade or otherwise,
be lent, re-sold, hired out, or otherwise circulated without the
publisher's prior consent in any form of binding or cover other than
that in which it is published and without a similar condition including
this condition being imposed on the subsequent purchaser.

Reading Level 1.6

Reprinted by arrangement with Penguin Putnam Inc.
10 9 8 7 6 5 4 3 2 1

CONTENTS

THE MOUSE

"What are you doing, Kate?" asked Digby.

"Shh," said Kate. "I am trying
to catch a mouse."
She sat very still
by a little hole in the wall.

"Why?" said Digby.

"Why do you want to catch a mouse?"

"I am a cat," whispered Kate.

"Cats catch mice.

Now please be quiet."

She stared at the hole.

"What will you do

with the mouse?" asked Digby.

He sat down beside Kate.

"Shh," said Kate. Her nose twitched.

Digby sighed. He was quiet.

Kate and Digby sat by the hole

for a long, long time.

No mouse came out.

They sat, and sat, and sat.

Finally Digby saw something move

in the hole.

A tiny head peeked out.

"Look!" yelled Digby. "A mouse."

The mouse popped back in his hole.

"Oh," said Digby. "He's gone."

Kate stood up and looked at Digby.

She looked angry.

"Now what are you doing, Kate?"

asked Digby.

"I am trying to catch a dog," said Kate.

"A very noisy dog.

And when I do, he will be sorry."

"Good-bye, Kate," said Digby.

"I will see you tomorrow."

Digby left in a hurry.

Kate sighed.

She sat down by the hole.

"Digby is my good friend," she said.

"But there are times

when a cat must be a cat—

alone."

LUNCH

"Something smells good," said Kate.

"I am making soup for lunch," said Digby.

"Vegetable soup."

"I love vegetable soup," said Kate.

"When will lunch be ready?"

"Soon," said Digby.

"Will you set the table, Kate?

I must stir the soup."

Kate set the table.

Digby stirred the soup.

Round and round. Round and round.

"Now will you pour the milk?" said Digby.

Kate poured the milk.

She did not spill a drop.

Digby stirred the soup.

Round and round. Round and round.

“Now we need sandwiches,” said Digby.

Kate got cheese and bread.

She made fat cheese sandwiches.

Digby stirred the soup.

Round and round. Round and round.

“How about dessert?” said Digby.

Kate put pudding in glass dishes.

She put whipped cream on the pudding.

Digby stirred the soup.

Round and round. Round and round.

"Is the soup ready?" asked Kate.

"Yes," said Digby.

He stopped stirring.

Digby and Kate ate vegetable soup

and fat cheese sandwiches.

They ate pudding with whipped cream.

They drank cold milk.

Everything tasted delicious.

Kate looked in the pot.

"There is more soup left," she said.

"Would you like some?" asked Digby.

"No thank you," said Kate.

"I am quite full.

You made a wonderful lunch."

"Thank you," said Digby.

"Now it is time to clean up, Kate.

Will you wash the dishes?"

"Oh, no," said Kate.

"You can wash the dishes, Digby.

It is *my* turn to stir the soup."

And she did.

Round and round. Round and round.

THE PAINT JOB

"Today I am going to paint the walls
in my house," said Digby.
"Oh good," said Kate. "I will help you."
"You are a good friend," said Digby.

Digby put on his painter's hat.

He started to paint.

He painted long, neat strokes.

Up and down. Down and up.

He worked carefully.

He finished one wall.

"Look, Kate.

Doesn't this wall look nice?" asked Digby.

"Yes, it does," said Kate.

"Look at *this* wall," she said.

"Oh my!" said Digby.

"Do you like it?" asked Kate.

"I have a special place for you

to paint," said Digby.

“This is fun,” said Kate.

“Yes,” said Digby.

He painted more long, neat strokes.

Up and down. Down and up.

"And when we are done," he said,

"your picture will look so nice on my wall."

PRETEND

Kate looked at her calendar.

"Oh my!" she said. "Summer is over.

It is the first day of fall.

The air will be cool,

and leaves will fall from the trees.

I will wear my new red sweater."

Digby came to visit Kate.

"Why are you wearing your new red sweater?"

asked Digby. "It is hot today."

"Look," said Kate.

"It is the first day of fall."

“Oh dear,” said Digby.

“I wanted to go to the beach today.

I wanted to swim and make sand castles

and eat ice cream.

Now what can we do?”

Kate and Digby sat down to think.

The sun was bright.

The air was hot.

"I know," said Kate.

"Let's play pretend.

We can pretend that it is summer."

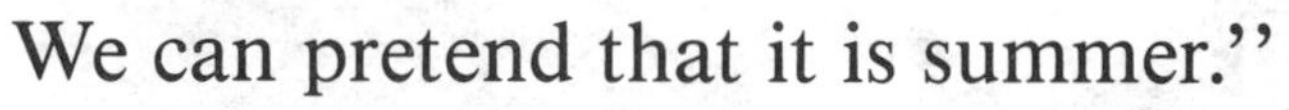

“Great!” said Digby.

Kate took off her new red sweater.

The two friends went off to the beach.

THE LETTER

One day Kate got a letter. It said:

Dear Kate,

Please come and visit me next week.

Bring whatever you will need.

Love,

Aunt Hazel

Kate showed the letter to Digby.

Digby said, “You can’t go.”

“Why not?” asked Kate.

“Because,” said Digby, “I would miss you.”

“You are a good friend,” said Kate.

“But Aunt Hazel is a good aunt.”

Digby sighed.

"I will be sad if you go," he said.

Kate looked at Digby.

She looked at the letter.

"I will be sad if I *go*," said Kate.

"And I will be sad if I do *not* go.

What can I do?"

Then Kate had an idea.

She got some paper.

She wrote a letter.

Dear Aunt Hazel,
I will come to
visit you.
I will bring Digby.
He is my friend.
I need him.
Love,
Kate

She showed the letter to Digby.

"Great!" said Digby.

"Let's pack."

THE PRESENT

Digby was at home.

"I want to give Kate a present," he said,

"because she is my friend.

But I do not know

what to give her."

Digby thought and thought.

"She likes mice,"

said Digby.

"But I cannot catch a mouse."

He thought some more.

"She likes vegetable soup,"

said Digby.

"But I cannot put vegetable soup

in a box."

He thought some more.

"She likes red sweaters,"

said Digby.

"But she already has one."

Then Digby had an idea.

He got a box.

He got pretty paper and a yellow ribbon.

He wrapped his present for Kate.

Then he took the present

to Kate's house.

“Hello, Digby,” said Kate.

She was holding a little box

behind her back.

“Here,” said Digby.

“This is a present for you.

Because you are my friend.”

Kate took Digby's box.

She opened it.

Inside was a bone.

"It is a bone," said Kate.

"Yes," said Digby.

"It was my favorite bone."

"Oh, thank you," said Kate.

"It is a wonderful present."

Then Kate gave Digby her little box.

"This is a present for you," she said.

Digby took the little box.

He opened it.

Inside was a red felt mouse.

"It is a red felt mouse," said Digby.

"Yes," said Kate.

"It was my favorite red felt mouse."

"Oh, thank you," said Digby.

"It is a wonderful present."

Kate chewed on her new bone.

Digby played with his red felt mouse.

They were happy together.

Because they were wonderful friends.